MY DREAM

SAFA KHATOON

XpressPublishing
An imprint of Notion Press

XpressPublishing
An imprint of Notion Press

No.8, 3rd Cross Street,CIT Colony,
Mylapore, Chennai, Tamil Nadu-600004

ISBN 978-1-63633-020-4

Nothing is impossible when we have a family.

Contents

ACKNOWLEDGEMENTS

I am Thankful to my life's super hero my dad. I would have not completed this story without his inspiring words that made me to write more about this story. I wrote this story just for a time pass but my dad's inspiring words brought this time pass story to publish.

I am Thankful to my best mom who supported me to complete this story. I am thankful to my supper naught brother who tried to copy my style and started to write a story about his adventure. Being a naught person he helped me thinking more about the story and so called hero of this story.

I would like to express my special thanks to the genuine human, motivator and guide my school's principal Mr M.H. PARAMESWARAN. Who is curiously waiting for this book?

I would like express the special thanks to my teacher cum best friend cum moral teacher Mr Devaraju. The person who listens to me even in his busy schedule. I am very glad to have such people in my life.

Suraj.B.R, The best classmate and the best elder brother that I have ever seen. He is a funny charter in my school life. He never used to take any topic serious. I felt thankful to the best person who entertained me by his funny nature when I was disappointed.

Vishwas, The best person in my school life. Who motivated me when he knew that I am writing a story? I am thankful to his beautiful short story of a tour in forest with the friends that took my entire tense mood away. I always recall the short story whenever I am tense.

I am thankful the fantastic person Pavan Kalyan. My best buddy. He is just like open book never hides anything a very much opened minded person who inspired me a lot. I am very glad to write this book by his inspiration and the best movement was when he brought me out of the reality and made me think something creative.

I am thankful to my best elder brother Siddeshwar. The person who always used to crake jokes even in the serious topics. He didn't even believe me when I said him I am writing a story. He is always naughty and his naughtiness made me write and prove that I have written a story.

I would like to express a special thanks to both of my real life super heroes my best Mamaji's. They just kept motivating me to complete this book as soon as possible and one more special thanks for listening to my story even though you they had no interest in it.

A special thanks to all my family members who gave me this idea to write a story. Their support and endless love made me to complete this book. I have no words to express their moral support and the endless love. Thank you all...

I feel so glad to have all wonderful moral supporters in my life. I really thank them because I never dreamt to publish this book. Now rest other things is left to you all I have just claim the first step and I am sure all you people will not let me lose the hope at the first step itself. I hope this book will bring some sort of interest those who read it.

PROLOGUE

"No one ever said am a different person in the universe. But I can prove it that

-Hero...

I never had a dream to become an all-rounder or perfect in everything. On the other hand I never had a dream fly all over the sky like a fairy. I had always a criminal dream. The dream always starts with criminal scenes. The case will be solved when a detective investigate about the case at last the case closes. People say there is nothing special in my dream but if somebody asks my opinion about my dream I say there each and everything is special and have some thrilling part too...

This story about the detective life...

The real story starts from here.

I

MY DREAM

I am a detective of supernatural, who never failed in solving cases. My dream made me to think so much when I knew that am not a hero of the dream wanted to who was that? One day a strange meet with strange hero who came in front of me with strange look and with hiding his face. Who never showed me his identity but became the team member of detectives of supernatural. The strange person changed my all techniques to solve cases. But whenever I ask him to introduced himself he runs away but never said me who is he? I didn't even know his name I kept calling him "Hero". I had always a hobby to sketch the imaginary world. Suddenly I got some message and some location I opened it. The message sender was hero and the location was my home building. I took my revolver and my smart watch and reached the location. Hero started questioning me how come you have reached the location so soon. My answer was it is my magic.

Hero: I have something very interesting to solve today...I am sure you will be excited to see what the case is?

Detective: yes I am excited to see...

Hero: Have a look on this case...

Detective: What! A box ...

Hero: yeah! We need to investigate about this box and to find out the history behind this box...

Detective: I think you have brought this box from one of the antic shop...

Hero: Oh! Madam observe this box properly it is a puzzled box.

Detective: So what can I do here...? Tell me.

Hero: I knew that you have a hobby of solving puzzles. I am trying to solve this box from morning

Till now I have not even able to solve and open it

Detective: Ok! Let me try once...

I took a slight look on to the puzzled box and started solving it. It took some 25 minute...to solve... The box started creating some nonsense wired voice. Hero suddenly entered my room with full alert and he started questioning me what that is wired voice I was not answerable because of box it was playing some wired music that was irritating our ears like a hell. Hero threw that box out of my room's window the box came back to my table I was laughing behind hero.

He turned towards me and gave a strange and serious look I said I would laugh anymore. I was looking at the box suddenly I found some symbol glowing on the box. I saw hero was irritated and sitting in the corner. I left him also and sat on table with box and magnified glass I saw there was some symbol like a tiger cub. I recalled myself that I have seen this tiger cub somewhere then I remembered that last year I participated in a drawing competition where I got a medal.

Hero: I am going I have some pending work I will be back in few minutes

Detective: Ok sure

I found that medal with very difficult then I saw that medal symbol is same symbol on box too...I placed the medal on the box where it was inserted the medal act like a key of the box and box was open. I found a paint brush and some papers I kept all the things aside and the box was empty. I took the paper that I got in box started shading slightly with a pencil where I got some number 4:00 AM it was a time. I shared a hero that I have got some time and a paint brush in a box by messaging him. He came to me very soon and started asking me so many questions about the box. Hero touched the paint brush all of the sudden the box started catching fire. I went near to paint brush the fire monster came out I was so close to the monster. Hero pulled me out and we went out through the window but my room was fully destroyed Hero took the rope tried it to window and said me to get down I reached the ground safely but the rope cut down and hero jumped from 2nd floor near from my window. He said here goes nothing and he jumped from there it was very dangerous jump. But he was safe when he reached to the ground I don't know how he is safe because I closed my eyes I didn't see. I asked him are you fine?

Hero: Oh! Madam open your eyes am fine standing here

Detective: How is it possible you are not injured after jumping from the 2nd floor?

Hero: Come on... I am a hero I have all supernatural powers that are not very easy to believe.

The box came to me down from my window and the fire was cut off. We reached my home it look normal as it had no fires at all everything was normal made a something mystery.

Hero: How is it possible? How the room and home is fine when we saw it had destroyed fully and it is fine now.

Detective: I think even am related to this case. Hero I got some time on some paper that I found in the box...

Hero started dancing after looking on to the time

Hero: It's time rock now.

Detective: What are you doing crazy? We are on duty right now ...

Hero: yes! I knew that I have some special watch. It can show us the past of the particular time.

Detective: What are you waiting for just go ahead

Hero sets the time on the watch. His incredible watch showed us some enact of some person is killed at 4:00AM I found the person's face...

Detective: Pause this enact now if you can Hero

Hero: Sure! But what happen?

He paused enact for me. I wanted to see the person's face so he zoomed the person's face... suddenly I shouted "Tommy"...

Hero: Wait! What! Tommy is it a dog?

Detective: No it is a person's name... I mean his name is "Ram charan"... He is one of my classmates

Hero: A person can't be named as Tommy... ok! Why did u remember him now?

Detective: Actually I found him in this enact he is killed at 4:00AM

Hero: Do you know now it is conformed this case is more related to you.

Hero resumed the enact we saw that Ram charan is killed for his profession.

Ram charan is a great artist who has say many stories is hidden behind a small painting. He had a magical paint brush...People were crazy to know that he has a magical paint brush...

Detective: Have you ever heard about the magical paint brush artist...?

Hero: Yep! I have heard somewhere about this magical artist. But I am not interested about it ...

Detective: The case is about the magical artist. The person is Ram charan

Hero was not listening to me just keeping quite looking out of the window...

Hero: Madam I think your table is messy let me help you out to clean...

Detective: Oh! Really I said you something a few minutes before did u hear that tell me...

Hero: Am very straight forward I didn't listen to you... fine

I stopped the argument with Hero and back to my table and what am I seeing the paint brush is glowing when I saw it with magnified glass it's the magical paint brush of Ram charan.

Hero: I am going home...

Detective: No! I mean see this I have shocking news here...

Hero: Tell me what happen?

Detective: I have Ram charan's magical paint brush with me.

Hero: Seriously! We will be in problem now right!

Detective: Right!

Hero was thinking too much about the paint brush and the problem ...Suddenly I got an idea like thought something different way...

Hero: We will bury the paint brush somewhere... where people can't reach

Detective: I think this magical paint brush's powers have killed Ram charan ... I mean to say like might this paint brush has so strong powers I think Ram charan wants to kill the powers. So Ram charan is killed by paint brush...

Hero: You wanted to convey me that Ram charan didn't wanted this paint brush should be killed and it shouldn't reach any evil person right!

Detective: yes you are right!

Hero: We need to investigate more about it right!

Detective: Yep! Ok we will investigate it...

Hero: Then what are you waiting for let us go now to Ram charan's house to know more...

Detective: Now! Are you crazy? It is late night Hero look at the time...

Hero: Keep quite now we are going to Ram charan's home...

Detective: Ok!

I said him ok but what to do I am really helpless because hero was not listening to me... we came out of my home and came down to basement.

Hero: Tell me where is his home?

Detective: No! Let me drive your car today...

Hero: Are you sure? Will you drive the car? Ok take the keys

Detective: Why question mark on your face?

When I stepped inside I got to know why hero was questioning me that is am sure can I drive his car because his cars has so many features and it may confuse so much...

Hero: What happen? Come on we are getting late...

Detective: Yep! Sure

I was driving the car Hero was laughing by looking some funny videos. I was irritated by it so I had a supper idea in my mind.

Detective: Excuse me Hero... We are on duty can you stop doing what you are doing actually?

Hero: Off course... not I am bored you are driving very slow...

Detective: Ok I will not change my speed limit am sorry.

Hero: Same here...

We reached painter's street and Ram charan's home...Hero was arguing with me I parked car in a parking lot and we reached the door step of the Ram charan's house. The door was open when I turned towards the home I really kept by quiet seeing the home it was similar to the chamber of horrors...

Hero: Tell me why you stopped arguing... Tell me.

Detective: Look the home Hero...

Hero: What!

Hero kept quite after seeing the house... Then he pulled me out and we were back to my home again...

Detective: What the hell? Why did you bring me back to the home...?

Hero: I felt like we will investigate tomorrow be ready morning sharp 8 mornings... I love punctuality. Good night ... see you tomorrow...

Detective: Good night!

Next morning.....

As per Hero said me he will be at 8 to go together to solve the case of Ram charan. But he didn't come at 8 when I saw the time it was all ready 9 I was waiting for him from past one hour. I made a call to the punctual person Mr Hero.

Hero: Hi morning...

Detective: Morning...

Hero: why did you call me? You know you have killed my lovely sleep.

Detective: Oh! Really do you remember what you said me yesterday night... you Mr punctual I am waiting for you from past 1hour...

Hero: Oh! Sorry I will be there in 10 minutes

Detective: Ok you have just 10 minutes.

As per his 10 minutes he didn't reach me it was already 10 o clock when he reached my home.

I welcomed him with a great smile... he was also smiling at me...

Detective: Do you know what the time is actually now? (Shouting)

Hero: Chill out madam it is just 10 why are you worried a lot ...?

Detective: Time is there to utilize not to waste...

Hero: I am sorry now let us go... please forgive me...

Detective: Ok! It's ok

Hero: let us go now...

Detective: Tell me did you have your breakfast?

Hero: Nope!

Detective: Ok I have brought something for you for your breakfast.

Hero: Oh! Thank you so much... I was really hungry

Detective: you're welcome....

I was driving the car and he started questioning again.

Hero: Yummy! It is really tasty breakfast... really today the day will be the best because the day is started with a yummy breakfast...

Detective: Thank you... I think you like it so much...

Hero: Not liked it I loved it

Detective: Sounds good...

Hero: Ok! By the way you never introduced yourself to me... may I know why?

Detective: Wow! Look who is asking this question...

Hero: Why?

Detective: Mr Hero did you introduced yourself to me...

Hero: Hmm... ok now we will introduce each other.

Detective: Oh! First you introduced.

Hero: No! I mean ladies first...

Detective: your bad luck we have reached the destination. The Ram charan's home now we are on duty we will introduce ourselves some other day...

We reached the Ram charan's house. The house look more wired then the night's look. We were confused I thought the home is the same or not but some of the name plate of the Ram charan confirmed that it is the same house... we stepped inside it was wired and I found some wild cats sculptures. Hero took next step by speaking to me that this home has 2 faces when he stepped inside the wild cats eyes were shining. I pulled him out of the home and he started shouting.

Hero: why did you pull me back say me... you have lost your mind I think...

Detective: Yes! You would have been lost the mind if u would go through this laser beams...

After seeing the laser beams Hero kept his mouth shut... he stepped back...

Hero: What can we do? How to go through these beams?

The lasers beams disappear we thought the beams are no more when I threw the pencil. It turned into hashes... the box was glowing I found an empty box has some paper in it. It was something like a clue it was...

If you want go safe from these beams throw this box in the middle and use these sheets to see all the dangerous beams...

I got a red coloured transparent sheet as we got the message by the box. We threw the box into the middle and by the help of the sheets we saw all the beams are arranged in a same line ends at the centre of the box...

Hero: I think this box is helping us...

Detective: It is helping but now what to do?

Hero: I will use my supernatural powers and reach the other side safely...

Detective Oh! Then what about me?

Hero: I will take you to the other side...

I was standing aside then suddenly I felt like someone is calling me for a help...I thought am just dreaming. But same sound came again to me.

Detective: Hero did you listen to any noise tell me...

Hero: No! What happen?

Detective: No nothing....

I kept quite because hero said he didn't listen to any noise but I could listen that someone is calling me for a help...

Hero: What happen you look little bit in tension...

Detective: I am not...

I hide the truth of that unknown voice calling for help... I begin to think why the voice is only avoidable to me...

Hero: Ok! Madam...Are you ready? To complete this task...

Detective: Yeah! I am ready.

Hero: Close your eyes and hold my hands...

Detective: Sure! But why am I supposed to close my eyes and hold your hands...

Hero: So that I can take you to the other side of the trap and so that you will know what my powers...are

Detective: Ok...

As he said I hold his hands and closed my eyes... Then he took that box and took me to other side of the trap. I could listen to the unknown voice calling me again and again. Hero was looking at me very seriously.

Hero: Are you alright you look little bit dull.

Detective: Hmm... Hero we will go back. This case will solve by anyone else we will drop it here itself...

Hero: Are you crazy? We are so close to the case. I am dam sure you want to complete this case but something is stopping you...

Detective: No Hero! Nothing is stopping...

Hero: As per I have seen your records you have never failed in any case or drop it in between... tell me why are you breaking your record by dropping your own classmate's case.

I kept quiet by listening to Hero I spoke to myself that should I hide the secrete of unknown or not my soul said you should be hide it.

Hero: come on... Speak up.

Detective: Hmm... Ok we will solve this...

Hero: That's sounds good... now lets us move forward...

Detective: Yes! Sure...

Suddenly my smart watch vibrates when I checked it the message has been arrived by the Ram charan's number. I began to think how Ram charan's number is active. I started reading the message was:-

You must be thinking how my number is active? As you know I have died because of my magical paintbrush I knew you are listening to some unknown voice calling you for a help too... don't get confused I will clear all your doubts...

Hero: Hey! What happen? You are standing with a shocking expression.

My response is zero... He pulled out my smart watch and started reading the message...

Hero: This is impossible... The person is dead. How the number is active... What is the matter of an unknown voice calling you for a help?

Detective: Hmm...

Hero: I think someone else using his number and sharing us this type of message.

Detective: But... this person knows even about the unknown voice calling me for a help...

Hero: Hey! But why didn't you say me about it.

Detective: I know you are angry about it...

Hero: No I am not. But you would have said me about it... Oh! Now I knew it why did you want to drop the case in between? Was it the reason or something else you are hiding partner?

Detective: Hmm... I have nothing to share you now. I have hid nothing else.

Hero: What is next?

Detective: Now we need to find out whether the Tommy's number is active or not.

Hero: So who we will help us out of this situation.

Detective: One of my team member and the best hacker can help us out in this situation.

I commanded my smart watch to call the team member the one who is very good in hacking...

Detective: Hey! Hi buddy hacker.

Hacker: Oh! Hi... How can I help you out?

Detective: So you know I need your help.

Hacker: Of course I knew it. I even know you are right now in Ram charan's house.

Hero: It is because of GPS tracker... That is there in our uniform behind the team logo. Am I right?

Hacker: yes! You are... who are you? The logo secrete is only knew to the team members.

Detective: Actually he is a new team member.

Hacker: How is it possible? I didn't know there is someone else in our team.

Hero: Now you got it. I am a team member. So can you verify is Ram charan's number is active or not...

Detective: Yes! Help us to know.

Hacker: I didn't like him. He is very straight forward and I think he is curious to know what next step...is

Hero: Buddy chill out I am not that kind of person.

Detective: you go just verify now!

Hacker: Ok! I will get you information as soon as possible.

Hero: Quick buddy we have no time.

Detective: Hero! Can you stop it?

I was irritated by listening to both of them. I shared hacker the message that, I got from Ram charan's number.

Few minutes...after

Some call on my phone. It is hacker...

Hacker: Hey! What is the matter of unknown voice calling you for the help?

Detective: I don't know in fact the voice is only audible to me.

Hacker: The number is not active from last Friday...

Detective: Last Friday but that day he had a flight to Italy for international competition.

Hacker: But... You dropped him airport right!

Detective: No he sent me a message that he will go to airport by his own transport so I said no issues.

Hacker: Isn't it strange...

Detective: What is strange here I couldn't find anything strange?

Hacker: I got the information from airlines that; tommy didn't travel though his ticket was booked.

Detective: Then where did he go? Must be he missed the flight.

Hacker: No! There is no ticket booked again for Tommy.

Detective: Where will he go?

Hacker: See all these CCTV footages. Tommy entire airport but didn't travel to Italy. How is it possible?

Detective: Then where did he go...? Check any private air crafts are there to the Italy.

Hacker: yea! I will check.

A few minutes later...

Hacker: No there were no private planes to the Italy on the same day. I have checked other planes passenger list his name is not there in other planes list also...

Detective: Wait a minute... I saw an enact of Ram charan killed for his magical paint brush.

Hacker: Share me that enact may be we will get when he is killed or where is he killed?

Detective: It's with Hero. I will share you.

I saw all around Hero was not there. Then I got message by Hero. I was sleepy by listening to you. So I came up to sleep. Share this enact to the Hacker.

Detective: Up? He went up to sleep. Where?

When lifted my head and looked up to the roof he is sleeping and floating as like the one floats in water. I shared Hacker the enact.

Hacker: This enact is done in the location India airport. The day is last Friday.

Detective: What about the message that sends to me by his number?

Hacker: It's Tommy only who shared you this message.

Detective: How is it possible?

Hacker: Chill out! You are thinking so much. Have look on this video.

Detective: Ok!

I could see the live video of Tommy. I rubbed my eyes and played the video again it was the same.

Hacker: You know actually Tommy is everywhere because of his magical paint brush.

Detective: You mean Tommy's life is in his magical paint brush.

Hacker: One main thing only we both can see him.

Detective: Only we can see him... is it because we are his classmates?

Hacker: No! Not because of that. But yes! I can say because we know the secret of his magical paint brush and a price less box.

Detective: Wait! A box. I have a box right now.

Hacker: Share me a snap now.

I shared the snap of the box. I was waiting for the reply and what I got the reply the box is same...

Detective: It is same box! But buddy I even have his magical paint brush.

Hacker: Did the box help you? You will have good adventurous case because both of them of supernatural powers.

Detective: Yes! The box helped me out 2 times. Let's see what adventure I will have in this case.

Hacker: The best adventurous case you are handling. All the best!

The conversation ends up with the hacker. I looked up Hero still resting. I felt so lazy person got all these powers he is using it for resting.

Suddenly he came down.

Hero: What did you say I am lazy?

Detective: Hey! When did I say you lazy?

Hero: Ok! You got any information from that person or simply you wasted 45 minutes of time.

Detective: Yep! I got enough information about the Tommy's flight to Italy and he said we will have a very adventurous case.

Hero: Oh! Really lets us see.

The box started glowing. Hero opened it he got a 2 maps of same kind...he gave me one and kept with him the other one.

We were moving forward then suddenly some wall came between us to save me from that wall he pushed me other side and what we were separated. Then I got it why did box give us the same kind of maps. Because the box knew it that we will be separated. I tried to contact Hero but the dammed signals were not there. I moved forward by referring the map. I got a message by Hero a voice note:

Hey! There is no network here. It is very difficult to contact each other and yes make sure your GPS tracker is on. Share me the hacker's number. I am fine here.

I shared him hacker's number. I was happy and relaxed to hear that he is alright. I was walking from past 30 minutes I didn't find anything. Then I found Tommy's gallery of paintings. I really got something very interesting. A beautiful family photo of Ram charan that was painted by him. It was made by all words and sentences. I felt very proud to be his friend because of his greatest talent. It was hard to believe but it was a true fact. I shared this image to Hacker and Hero. Hero shared his voice note to me:

Hero: Unbelievable! Fantastic piece of art.

I was happy to hear all the things Hero said. Then I moved forward looking his all piece of arts. I heard some voice behind me when turned towards. What I am seeing Tommy is in front of me.

Ram charan: Hey! Hi Buddy.

Detective: Hi... Hi! Tommy I mean Ram charan.

Ram charan: It's ok! You can call me as "Tommy".

Detective: Ok!

Ram charan: I know you have so many questions.

Detective: actually I am thinking from where I shall start from asking you my question.

Ram charan: You just be cam I will clear your all doubts.

Detective: Ok! Tell me what is the matter of the unknown voice calling me for a help?

Ram charan: You will know it very soon.

Detective: Answer me something Tommy so that I concentrate on the case it is disturbing me.

Ram charan: Don't force me. You will know why is it happening?

Detective: Ok! As you wish but remember I will find out what is the reason behind it?

Ram charan: I have come here to say you what is going to happen next?

Detective: If am not wrong your life is in you magical paint brush.

Ram charan: Yes! But this full moon day is special. After this full moon day my life span and magical powers of this paint brush gets over.

Detective: Can I do anything? I mean like can I save your magical paint brush's powers? So that I can save you.

Ram charan: Yes! You can do but there is a risk in it.

Detective: Tell me I can do it for you.

Suddenly Tommy disappear I searched him in that gallery. Then I found him in his self-pot rate painting. He came out the painting. I felt like I am seeing a 3D movie.

Ram charan: no buddy you can't save magical paint brush and me after today's night.

Detective: Then it means you will be never back.

Ram charan: No I may come when you complete this case.

Detective: Ok!

Ram charan: Solve this case very soon so that you know who is Hero?

Detective: Wait a minute! I didn't tell you about Hero. How did you know him?

Ram charan: I know him... Ok! My time is up. I just wanted to say find my dairy you will know what your next task is.

Detective: Task! But Tommy...

Ram charan went away I don't know what was happening because I heard something new that Tommy knows who is Hero? I thought of asking hacker do he know who is Hero. I asked him by sending my voice note:

Hey buddy do you know who is Hero?

His reply killed me because even he knows who is Hero? What was happening? Being my best classmates they didn't say me who am this Hero? I kept thinking about it and moved forward then I got Ram charan's room when I opened the door some wired noise came out of the room. I got Hero over there. He was busy in searching the details of Ram charan he messed up all the room by searching clues. I was seeing all this what he has messed up suddenly some voice came from behind. Hero kept the revolver near my head.

Hero: Hey! Who are you? What are you doing here?

Detective: Chill out dude! It's me...

Hero: Oh! Madam Detective. I am extremely sorry I was little bit alert that's it.

Detective: It's our duty to be alert don't worry I would also done the same if I would be in your place. It is my mistake that I didn't inform you that I am there in this room.

Hero: Hmm...

Detective: But Hero! Did you find any diary of Ram charan? We will know what's our next task is after reading the diary.

Hero: Yes! I remember I saw there is a locker in a study table. I thought off breaking it...

Detective: If you would have break the locker this magical home would finish us.

Hero: Really this home is horror of chamber. Everything us something magic in it. See this I got some key while I rushed up in Ram charan's his study table draws.

Detective: Ok! Frist we need to find his diary... Quickly!

Hero: Ok! You know the password of this locker.

Detective: I think yes...

I try to entire the password 1xxxxxxx... the password was right the locker opened successfully. I got his dairy in it. The box started glowing and the paint brush was also glowing. Slowly some voice came out of the box when I took the box in my hands. The box started reading Tommy's Dairy. Hero and I were listening to the dairy.

30 minutes later...

The diary was completed and our task was to take the magical paint brush to the magical world that is there in the magical price less box.

Detective: Hero... come on stand with me.

Hero: Ok!

Detective: "A prince of magical world. I request you to open the doors of magical world".

The box increased its size and said us to jump in it. We jumped together in to the box.

10 minutes later...

We reached the beautiful magical world. It was very pleasant and peaceful surroundings. I saw some forest as per the dairy we need to go to the magical forest I stepped inside the foggy forest.

Detective: Come on Hero! We have no time to enjoy all this peaceful surroundings.

Hero: I am coming.

Hero tried to step inside the forest but some magical powers stopped him to go inside. I couldn't understand why was it happening?

Detective: Hero something is stopping you to step inside. Ok! I have an idea hold my hand we will step together...

Hero: Ok!

As I said we both did the same we were able to go through the foggy layer to entre inside the forest. The forest was so beautiful. It had all cherry blossom trees... all over the forest pink leaves. The forest was welcoming us by putting up a flowers carpet. I really felt like I am a queen of this forest and everyone is welcoming me. Hero started questioning me...

Hero: Why did it happen? You crossed the foggy layer but why can't I?

Detective: I think it may be because of paint brush or the price less box.

Hero: Did you meet Ram charan?

Detective: Yep! Actually he said me about his dairy...

Hero: Hey! When did you meet him? You didn't say me about it.

Detective: because only I can see or listen to him. You can't see him. Ah! Now I got it why did Tommy separate us?

Hero: Yes! Even I got it. He thought if you will be speaking to him and if I can't find him I will think you are mad so he separated us.

Detective: Yes! True.

Hero: Ok! Did he say you what is the matter of a unknown voice calling you for a help.

Detective: I don't know. He said I will know it very soon.

I said Hero whatever I spoke to Ram charan. He was very curious to listen what is next?

Hero: So you mean to say is this pain brush and Ram charan will have no powers and life span after this full moon day.

Detective: Yes!

Hero: What is next? Because we are just walking and walking...

Detective: Actually hacker told me this box will bring us in lots of trouble so just stay alert.

Hero: Ok!

Detective: As per dairy we need to reach the magical river.

Hero: Wow! A magical river.

Suddenly I found the fire monster the same monster that I found in my room earlier. I said Hero about the monster. Unfortunately monster saw Hero and attacked on him. I came in front of monster.

Fire monster: Oh! You are back. My honour to see you again.

Detective: What!

Fire monster: You are the creator of the magical world.

Detective: No I am just a detective. I have come here to solve the Ram charan's case.

Fire monster: You are re- born.

Detective: If I am the creator of this world. Then why did you attack him?

Fire monster: I am sorry he was a stranger and I thought he will harm this world so...but I am sorry again he can't be cure.

Detective: What? You can't say me this that he can't be cure. Is there is no magic to cure him at least to some extent.

Fire monster: There is only way to save him.

Detective: What is that?

Fire monster: You have all the magic in your hands. But I am not 100% sure that he will recover.

Detective: Let me test "Oh! Beautiful magical world your creator is wishing you to cure this person"

I could see the magic worked only little bit it just cure the Hero's injury on his head and he was not in conscious. I thought no other way. I remembered that magical river will help me out.

Detective: Can you take him to the magical river? I will follow you.

Fire monster: Sure! I will take him to the river.

Fire monster took Hero to the magical river then I followed them. I reached there in 5minutes and what I am seeing so beautiful view of river. Very pleasant environment. Fire monster made Hero to lay down I bought some magical water from the river.

Detective: Come on Hero you can't leave this case in between. Get up Hero...

Fire monster: Yes! Get up gentleman.

I sat with Hero the same place. He was slowly opening his eyes and when he saw monster in front of his eyes he started screaming.

Hero: I will finish you monster. How dare you attack me?

Detective: Thank god you are cured.

Hero: Madam this place is not safe for us and this monster will attack on us again let us run from here now.

Detective: Clam down Hero! The fire monster will not harm us.

Hero: Let us run from here.

Detective: Oh my god! Hero I am serious it will not harm us.

Fire monster: I am extremely sorry sir I didn't know that you are with the creator of this magical.

Hero: Ok! Who is that? Do I know that person?

Detective: Hero...It's me.

Hero: Are you serious?

Detective: Yep! I am.

Fire monster: The magical palace is waiting for yow from several years.

Hero: So she is your world creator. Then you don't think she must have magical powers.

Fire monster: Yep! She has all over the control throughout this magical world.

Hero: Then she is the creator of this world.

Detective: Hero can you stop questioning the fire monster.

Hero: Ok! Now I can't walk anymore.

Detective: I may help, Hey magical forest can you take us to the magical palace.

Some of the magical horses came to me and they took me and Hero to magical forest. I really felt I am actually dreaming because all those things like magical horse and those imaginary magic. We reached the magical palace. I can see people made a great welcome with all flowers and with lots of enjoyment. People of the magical forest were happy to see me. All of them took me and Hero to the beautiful palace I had a very beautiful royal look.

Hero: Ah! Madam we need to know what is secret of unknown voice and what about?

Before I could reply Hero that, I don't know about it. Some body answered from a group of people.

Unknown person from group: The unknown voice is the soul of the forest that brought the magical world creator to the right place.

Detective: Who is it? Can you step forward from the group?

Unknown person: Hey! Sister it your lovely brother "Farhan". I think you don't remember me?

Detective: Farhan! How come you are here?

Farhan: Sister... I saw you on that day when you got Tommy brother's case you slept on your table by writing a clues what you got from magical paint brush and about the box. So I decided to come here and being the prince of this world people took great care and I was the person calling you for the help.

Detective: Then you are the person who brought me here to this world? How is it possible, How can I be the creator of this imaginary world?

Farhan: Chill out sister! You are the creator have a look on this video.

Some screen came in front of me and guess what I found in it Ram charan in it.

Ram charan: Hello...Hi... Farhan I know your sister is too much surprised by her seeing her surprise gift given by me as she remember I said she will have a surprise. Now I know she does not believe that she is creator of this beautiful world. Actually she took my magical paintbrush instead of taking her paint brush on the competition day and that day she drew all the imaginary that she is seeing now and guess what she don't even know she used my magical paint brush. The magical powers created this world. Hope at least she will believe now.

Detective: It means I have paintings became my magical world just because I used Tommy's magical paint brush.

Farhan: Today this paint brush will die. There is some special prayers for this paint brush so that you save it today.

Detective: You mean I should reach the magical temple.

Farhan: Yes! I will tell Hero to join us.

Magical horses took me to the magical temple where all the people were waiting for me to start the special prayers. I stepped inside the magical temple there I couldn't open my eyes because of some light. When I saw what was it? It is a beautiful crown it was shining so bright that I couldn't open my eyes when I stepped inside the temple. Some people started cheering:

Some unknown person: This temple was always waiting for you and today it is a time to give you all responsibilities of this crown and this beautiful world.

Detective: But! I don't belong to this world. I just came here to investigate about the my friend's case. I...I didn't even know I have create this world. My small mistake crated this world. I am sure I will not let the world to destroy but I can't take your responsibilities. I need to return back to the reality.

Some unknown person: you will be able to return back to the reality though you are the queen of this world. Your soul will be always here if there is something wrong here. The soul will bring you again. Now you have to take all these responsibilities.

Farhan brought a crown in front of me and he made me to ware it. I got all magical powers and I could see happiness in the eyes of the people. I got all the responsibilities my magic made magical paintbrush alive. I could see people wanted to celebrate they all started to decorate the palace everybody was busy with their own works. Farhan took me to the special river and said:

Farhan: Sister! You be here. May this view will take out your entire stress mood.

Detective; Hmm....

I sat there near the river and looking on to river water. I felt like river water wanted to convey me something. It was trying to tell me something that I couldn't understand. Hero came to me suddenly he kept his hand on my shoulder and I kept revolver ready and turned towards him full alert.

Hero: Oh! My god you will kill me today.

Detective: I'm... I'm extremely sorry. I was thinking something.

Hero: You are somewhere to be lost. What happen are you alright?

Detective: No! I am not alright! I don't know what is it happening and after owning these responsibilities I don't know what this magical world wants to convey me?

Hero: This River has something special Farhan said me. May your magic be able to make us know what is it trying to convey us?

Detective: I...I don't know

Hero: Just try once I am dam sure that your magic will work here.

Detective: Hey magical world tell me what you want to convey me? Tell me!

My magic didn't work here. Everything was normal the river water was flowing normally I didn't feel that river wants to convey me something. Farhan came to me and said:

Farhan: All the decoration is done. Come on it is time for you for a surprise party.

Hero: Yep! I was hungry. What is the time now?

Farhan: Oh! Hero here your watch doesn't work here.

Hero: What do you mean?

Farhan: If you have stay here in this magical world for whole 1day in reality world's time it is only 1 hour.

Hero: Wow! Very slow time it is.

Farhan: Come on it is lunch time.

Magical horses took us to the dining hall. Everyone welcomed me to the beautiful royal dining hall. It was so beautiful I could find the table was made up of clouds very soft same way the chairs were made up of clouds. People served food it was very delicious and tasty desert. Then I came out of the dining hall and sat in the gallery of the palace. I started thinking if I have brought the paint brush life back then I can even bring Ram charan's life back too with my powers. I thought off thinking about it and then I found Farhan.

Detective: Farhan I wanted to know something from you. Can you please tell about it?

Farhan: About what?

Detective: As I have brought the magical paintbrush life back. Can I bring the Tommy's life back too?

Farhan: No you can't do it so.

Detective: I have all magical powers around this whole magical world.

Farhan: Yep! I believe it. But if you try to bring him back this beautiful magical world will destroy it self.

Detective: But bhai...Is there is no other way to bring him.

Farhan: Being the creator of this world you can't be the reason of the end of this world. I just wanted to convey you this rest is up to you.

Detective: Ok! Let me think about it.

Farhan left me in gallery alone and as he said I was thinking about it. I kept thinking very deeply suddenly Hero came to be and pulled me and brought me to magical temple. I am seeing the soul of the magical forest, the soul of fire and the soul water. All those souls were trying to destroy it self.

Farhan: If you keep see this disaster we will not survive. Do something we have to rescue people. I will take all people to the palace these souls can't destroy the palace.

Hero: Ok! Then you take everyone to the palace. I will see what I can do here?

Detective: I think we need to find what is the reason behind this disaster?

Hero: We have no time for it to find out. Now we have to fight against the souls.

Detective: Ok!

I said Hero ok. But entire intension was to find what the reason behind this disaster was? Nature is not so cruel that it will destroy itself. There is something made these souls to get angry and destroy itself. I saw the river it was flowing beyond its flowing speed I went near the special river and tried to know the reason for this disaster. I reached the river and started asking why is happening.

Detective: Tell me magical river. Why is it happening? Do I have commit some mistake or the reason is something else. Tell me it is very important to save this world.

I lost the hope of saving this world. I decided to fight against the souls. Some voice came from behind me.

The river water: I'm sorry I wanted to convey this when you asked me for the first time itself. I couldn't able to because of that person who gave you an idea to use your magic.

Detective: Seriously! Ok now you tell me what is the reason behind this?

The river water: It is because of the paint brush the life span.

Detective: it means I wouldn't bring its life back.

The river water: Yep! No there is only way to bring peace in this world is to find that magical pearl. You will find it in my water so you will have 10 minutes to bring the pearl and bring peace and harmony back to this world. So your magic will help you to find the pearl soon.

Detective: Ok the pearl is in water.

The river water: Yes! You can't waste the time jump into the water quick.

I had no time to think what to do? When I have the reason then why to waste the time?

Detective: I am ready.

The river water: One more thing you can breathe inside the water because of your magic and your 10 minutes starts now.

I went inside the river water it was very deep usually the rivers are always deep. I could able breathe and see clearly then I started finding that pearl. It brought me very difficulties. When looked at my watch 5 minutes were done I had only 5 minutes more to bring the magical pearl. At last I found the magical pearl behind some glowing fish. I had only 2 more minutes to go out of the river water I took the pearl I started swimming back to the land somebody pulled me down. I came inside the water with the pearl it was the magical pearl's bodyguards. They tried to stop me.

Bodyguards: You can't take this magical pearl out of this special water.

Detective: This world is in trouble it is destroying itself. I need to take this pearl out.

Bodyguards: Who are you?

Detective: I'm there the creator of this world now let me go I have 1mintue 40seconds more to get out of this water.

Bodyguards: Yes! You may go now because I have verified that this magical pearl is going in the safe hands not in the evil hands.

Detective: Bye. Thank you for this magical pearl.

I had only 30 seconds more I should swim back to the land quick. I reached the land in 28 seconds only 2 seconds were remaining and I completed my task.

The river water: I appreciate you are you completed this task on time. Congratulations now you can save this world.

I reached magical temple then I saw Hero was totally injured lying down. He is completely injured by fighting against the souls. I quickly without wasting my time I took the magical paintbrush out and kept the magical pearl with it.

Detective: Hey! Magical world clam down... it is my mistake I brought the magical paintbrush's life back. Forgive your creator and stop disaster please...

The magical pearl started glowing and the paintbrush was losing its shine. It means the magical pearl was trying to suck all the life span of the magical paintbrush. The magical paintbrush was an evil that tried to bring this magical world's end. But the magical world brought the magical paintbrush to the end. People were safe in the magical palace. People came out of the palace and thanked me to save their life. I brought Hero to the magical river to cure his injuries with the help of magical horse. I made him lay down near the river bank and brought some water to him by my magical powers. I started applying the water to his injuries so that it cures soon. Hero was not in conscious I had an idea I thought now Hero is not in conscious let me see who is he by removing out his mask. Before I could take his mask out he opened his eyes and I couldn't see who is he?

Hero: I am feeling better.
Detective: Hmm...
Hero: How did you stop everything tell me.

Detective: I found what was the reason behind this disaster?

Hero: That's sounds cool. Then tell me the entire thing what has happen actually.

I started to tell him everything what happen in the river and etc...

Hero: Why nobody wants me to be part of this case I am also the member who is solving this case?

Detective: Hero's statement made me think why is it happening? Tommy spoke to me when Hero was separated by me? River didn't say me anything when Hero was with me? The same things happen in the river's case also. Why?

Hero: Oh! Hello madam lost again somewhere.

Detective: Don't you feel strange?

Hero: What can I feel strange here?

I felt first I should go in deep and bring out secrete behind it. I think now it is not important to speak anything with Hero right now.

Hero: Again lost somewhere.

Detective: No! I am here. Let us go back to the palace. You should rest now.

Some magical horses took us to the palace. We reached the palace. Farhan took Hero to his room and made him rest there.

Farhan: Hero! You are so brave hats off to you.

Hero: Brave for what?

Farhan: You have very hard injuries but your bravery is not losing the hope at all.

Hero: No buddy I have learnt it from your sister.

Farhan: Really!

Detective: Hey! Boys what is going on you both are whispering something tell me.

Hero: Nothing...

Farhan: Nothing we are speaking...

Hero: Hmm... Hey madam! I need some coffee can you get it for me

Detective: Sure... I will get it for you.

Hero and Farhan were whispering. They changed the topic when I asked them. I was just hiding and listening to them. But Hero found me.

Hero: Don't worry you no need to hide and listen to us. What we are speaking? I just said him all story of Ram charan's case.

Farhan: Yep! What a thrilling case di...

Detective: Hmm...

Hero: you don't need to be worried your bro is with me.

Farhan: Chill out di...! Hero is just like me. You don't worry I will be with him until and unless he completely cures.

Detective: Hmm...

I just believed them. But I planned something to bring what is the truth out without their knowledge.

Hero: I am hungry. What is the time? Dinner is ready or what?

Farhan: Oh! Wait for 10 minutes I will get you your tasty dinner.

Detective: No! Its ok Farhan... you stay here with Hero. I will get both of yours dinner here.

Farhan: So sweet of you di...

I came out of the room they stared speaking something again. I reached kitchen.

Detective: Chef! Is the dinner ready?

Chef: Oh yes! It is...

Detective: Ok! Can you serve Hero and Farhan?

Chef: Yes! Sure.

I came again to the room to see what there are doing? They were laughing loudly and then Hero found standing on the door.

Hero: Hey! What are you doing there? Come on let us have dinner together.

Farhan: Oh... Di! Come on we will have dinner together.

Detective: Hmm...

Hero: Hey! Stop giving a strange look. Smile please

Detective: Ok!

I smiled because Hero said me to and I could see he was happy with Farhan. We had dinner together and after the dinner. Farhan and Hero wanted to sit in the gallery.

Detective: So... I am leaving. Farhan it is your responsibility to take care of him. Sleep on time good night!

Hero: Wait a minute Madam... Can you permit me to...?

Detective: What permission you need from me?

Farhan: Actually di... Hero wanted to go explore the magical world so he is asking you.

Detective: What is your plan? Going out for whole day and when do you want to go?

Hero: Hey!

Farhan: Di... tell me will you permit us or not?

I thought for a while then I thought if Hero will go out for sometimes then I will be able to focus on the plan.

Farhan: Di... Can we go?

Detective: Yep! You guys have fun.

Hero: Wow! Thank you... thank you so much.

Farhan: Ok! Hero we will start from the Magical world's amusement park.

Hero: Wow! Thank you so much madam you permitted me to go out.

Detective: No it's ok. So you will have good enjoyment. Now sleep it's already late you both should get up early in the morning for your magical world's tour.

Farhan: Good Night!

Hero: Good Night!

I made one more to know what Farhan and Hero is speaking secretly.

Next morning...

I helped Farhan to pack the bag and very secretly without Farhan's knowledge I kept a small voice translator. Hero brought a map of the magical world and then they started their journey to explore the magical world. I was very happy to listen what my so called brother Farhan and Hero is speaking.

Hero: I am really surprised so easily she permitted me to go out.

Farhan: My sister is quite strict. But I am also thinking how come she said ok so soon.

Hero: Buddy we have come out to explore stop thinking about it.

Farhan: I'm hungry I need something to eat. Oh! I remember di... has packed some sandwiches. Would you like to eat?

Hero: Sure!

Farhan: Continue your story.

Hero: Hmm...

Farhan: I'm actually thinking how it is possible she didn't recognize you.

Hero: I know she will catch me one or the other day.

Farhan: I don't think so. Being her classmate she didn't recognize you.

Hero: Yep! She didn't. But before I say her something she will find me very soon.

I heard all the conversation held between Farhan and Hero. I was thinking who is that my classmate and if Hero is one of my classmate then why is he hiding his identity to me. If he is my classmate then how...How I couldn't recognize him. I could listen what Farhan is speaking to Hero. I was even trying to find out what was the relation between magical paint brush and magical world's disaster. I reached the special river I felt the river can help me out of this.

The river water: Oh! You are back.

Detective: Yep! You know that I will come back to you.

The river water: Absolutely I will know you will be back because you need to know what the relation between paint brush and the disaster is.

Detective: Yep! You know everything then why didn't u tell me before...

The river water: I wanted you think about it and come to me and ask about.

Detective: Hmm... Now tell me from beginning.

The river water: This whole thing is started with you only... One day you accidently used the power full magical paint brush for your competition because of your strong imagination this world was created to fight again the evil scoundrel people who wanted to use the magical paint brush in wrong ways. To stop them this world was created and we gave you all this world's responsibilities because you are the one who gave an idea to get rid of the evil people. We are successful to save magical paint brush in this world's magical temple. But unfortunately the magical paint brush had turned evil. The only thing that can control the evil things is this magical pearl. I wanted you to know about the magical pearl. So... if you really want to save this world you need to have this magical pearl with you every time. Take this magical pearl and one more thing I wanted you to say to know more about this magical pearl you have to go to the same place from where you brought the magical pearl out...

Detective: So after all I got something that can help me to save this world.

The river water: Take this map and have a happy journey. Successfully complete the task all the best! One more thing you can connect to me.

Detective: Thank you for your best wishes.

As per the map I have to go and find some more secret of the magical pearl.

The river water: Are you ready?

Detective: Yep! I am.

When I was stepping in the water the river stopped me.

The river water: Hey! Stop where are you going? You have to go inside the map with the help of the magical pearl.

Detective: What? Are you serious?

The river water: Yes I am.

Detective: Ok! You mean that secret of this magical pearl is in the map and my journey is in this map. Wow!

The river water: All the best!

This magical world is really strange I thought I will refer this map and go find the secret but here it is strange I am inside the map. Very difficult to believe it but I was actually in the map.

After 30 minutes...

I reached some desert area. Usually we have heard desert area have high temperature and all day sunny but here I found everything strange. The view was like the desert area but the temperature is not high. When I check weather report in my smart watch it had only 30 degree Celsius. Very strange desert that I would ever see in reality I could see nothing the place was empty. I was just walking and walking then after walking for so long distance. I found a hill I felt at least after walking for so long I got some hill. Now I have to claim it.

The river water: Yes! You have to claim it.

Detective: Really I have to claim it. Wait! How did you know I am thinking about to claim the hill.

The river water: It is because of the magical pearl locket I can able to know what exactly you are thinking.

Detective: Ok! Can you tell me why this desert area is strange with very cool climate?

The river water: Hmm... it is your imagination. How can I say why is the desert has the cool climate.

Detective: Oh my goodness! Now don't tell me that I have even created this desert like this.

The river water: Yep! You are the creator of this desert too. Let me clear you questions.

Detective: Please erase all this riddles.

The river water: Remember once you made a painting of the desert area and accidentally your brother Farhan spelled all water on the canvas.

Detective: Yep! I remember so How is it related to this? I used my normal paint brush not the magic one. Then how is this strange desert created.

The river water: You made the desert canvas before the completion or after it.

Detective: After the competition. Oh my goodness it means some of the magical power transferred into me when I used the magical paint brush and when I tried to dry up the canvas. I mean I touched it so the powers created even this strange desert.

The river water: Exactly! Right!

Detective: This desert is really strange. If I am not wrong the hill is made because I tried to dry the canvas with a cloth causes some designs appear that actually looked similar to the hills.

The river water: You can do it. Now you knew that this is your own painting you can easy reach the destination.

Detective: Hmm...

I felt I am traveling all my imaginary painting arts to know all the secret of the Tommy's case. Really I never expected this when I saw enact and started solving Tommy's case. I tried to claim up at last I reached the up. I was fully tied I couldn't able to walk more. When I looked to my left I found a city. I found some air craft was flying in the sky. They can't see me from very higher altitude. I have to do something so that they can know someone wants help. I had very nice idea I took my revolver and fired up to the sky. Thank god they came down to help me. I entered the city and guess what it is my own painting again a future world. I stepped inside the world everybody noticed me and welcomed me the same way I had welcomed in magical world. But the only difference was there human welcomed me in magical world and here the supper sonic robots and some humans. I was took the very beautiful 7 star hotel. Really amazing entry I had with the band and by giving me such sweet dishes to have. I wanted to click pictures with all the décor and tasty food.

After 10 minutes...

I tasted every special tasty dishes of the future world. Some of the girls took me to the place it was very peaceful. I was enjoying the peaceful environment.

The river water: Hey you have not come here to enjoy. You have to go and find the secret. Get up!

Detective: Ok! I am going...

I was lost in enjoyment. I wanted to go find about everything. One of the girl was shock to see the magical pearl locket.

The unknown girl: You know there is a very big secret behind this pearl.

Detective: What? Really! I am sure you will help me out of this.

The unknown girl: Come with me I will show a you my all books and research notes to find this magical pearl.

The unknown girl took me to her home and there she took me to secret room there I found her name Lisa. She was in search of this magical pearl. I found some book about this magical pearl. I took the book out of the shelf and the book was really very old.

Detective: Hey! This book's condition is not so good.

Lisa: 2 months ago while construction of this house was held I got this book in soil while digging. When I tried to open the book. The had only empty pages I used candle to find may there is something in it. But I was failed so I started searching this pearl.

Detective: Ok! I have an idea. I think this pearl's light will show us something. Let's try once.

Lisa: Ok! We will try.

I took out the magical pearl locket and slowly moved on the page of the book slowly the fonts were visible. It was someone's handwriting...I felt like it is someone's diary. The unknown girl started reading it.

Lisa: Dear Diary... Today is 31st March and I am very glad to write that I have successfully completed the experiment of the magical pearl. The pearl and this diary is incomplete with each other. Now I am glad no one can read my secret diary without the pearl's light.

Detective: Hey! We didn't get any clue from first page let us move on to second page...

I did the same I moved the locket slowly on the pages no fonts appear. I was shocked because the locket was not working... I turned the next page and used the same trick but it didn't work.

Lisa: I have an idea let us try it from the last page of the book.

Detective: Yep! May it work...?

I moved the locket in the last page of the book. I found some fonts were appearing I started reading them.

Detective: If accidentally somebody got my locket and the diary they can be able to read only first page. #my super trick.

Dear Diary... Today 2ndApril I made an experiment but failed in it. I wanted to change my paint brush into a computer paint brush. But I really found something different from my expectations. This paint brush can bring life in a non-living thing also. This paint brush has some magical powers too... I hope I will keep this magical paint brush safe from all scoundrels.

Lisa: I wish I would touch that magical paint brush.

Detective: It will give you lots of the trouble. Because of this magical paint brush I am here to find the secret behind it.

Lisa: It means you are the person whom we were waiting for. From the date this future world was created. I am very much hounded to see you live.

Detective: Oh my goodness not again... let us move to the next page.

Lisa: Ok! I will read this time... Dear Diary...Today is 4thApril today there was attack on me. Because of the magical paint brush. But I was shock to see myself standing without any injury. Then I knew that the locket is saving me from all the attacks. I really don't know what is going on in my life...Sometimes I really feel like somebody is calling me for help every time I feel something strange. I saw yesterday the paint brush was glowing again and again so I got some box it was normal puzzle box I made an experiment and made that normal box into the magical box. I kept the magical paint brush in the box and with the help of some people I tried to bury it. But I felt if somebody opens it their life will be trouble so I took the box and put it in the fire. I think the box has destroyed now I am not getting all strange sounds like before I used to listen.

Detective: My god! Whatever I found till now is created by this person.

Lisa: It means you have seen all these things.

Detective: Yep! I have come here to find the reason behind the creation of all these things. Now I have to find the relation between all these things. Now it's my turn to read what is there in the next page.

Lisa: Then I will move the locket on the page.

Detective: Dear Diary... Today is 6th April I thought I have destroyed the box but I was wrong the box was in my store room. The box was creating some wired sounds. I am worried what to do now I think I have to bury the box. I took the box and tried to bury it. I am very afraid I couldn't sleep tension free or I can't even say somebody about it.

Lisa: My god this magical paint brush is turning evil...

Detective: Lisa did you notice something. There is one day gap between every diary note.

Lisa: No actually as per reality you can say there is one day gap in between each note as per this future world it is right.

Detective: How?

Lisa: Let me clear you. In reality world there is 30 days in April right!

Detective: Yep! Ah! I understood... like the months have 30 days in reality in this world 15 days. In reality if some months have 31 days here in this world you will have 16 days. In the months you have 15 days you follow even number in the month you have 16 days you will follow odd number.

Lisa: Yep! You are right!

Detective: So I even had the same experience when I tried to open that magical box.

Lisa: Hmm... interesting

Detective: So lets us find the person's name. It is very important to find the person's name...

Lisa: We will open the middle page and try to find because this person had written the diary from last page may be this person have written the name in middle page.

Detective: Yep! Might be... let us see once.

Lisa: My god I got the name... look at the end of the page.

Detective: Tommy! Oh yes I forgot about him...But as I know about him. He is just a great artist is all this happen with him I never knew all this about him.

Lisa: Ok! We have revel the entire secret by his diary... let us go back to the page we were reading.

Detective: Ok! Now you have read the diary.

Lisa: Dear Diary... today is 8thApril. I think this magical paintbrush will kill me by torturing me day and night. I am unable to get rid of this magical paintbrush. Now only god can help me out of this situation. So I have kept something in this pearl locket. Hope if somebody accidently open they will what made me to become an artist.

Detective: Really! I have this locket from so many days but I didn't observe the locket can be opened...

Lisa: Let us see what secret does this locket revel....

We tried to open the locket but we were failing again and again... I found something was written on the locket. I took my magnified glass tried to observe what is written over...

but Lisa stopped me from behind...

Lisa: Stop! Don't open it...

Detective: But! Why Lisa?

Lisa: We didn't complete this page have look on the page. He has written in the end, the person will be in risk whoever opens this locket weather knowingly or unknowingly. They will know the secret of all my history with magical paint brush...

Detective: We have no option Lisa... its ok we are ready for taking risk. Wait let me see what is written on this locket. "Your life is in your hands"

Lisa: What are you saying? Let me see properly...

Detective: Ok!

Lisa: "You have risk to open this locket" you have read some different sentence but here it is written different.

Detective: Must be some trick or a warning to not open the locket.

Lisa: Hope So...

Detective: let us open it.

I tried to open again but the same way I was fail again...I simply kept the locket on my palm. It was glowing...and opened itself... played some video in front us there it was Tommy's home so many secret was revel I was really shock... we were in the Tommy's home but still I didn't know about all these how? I got a voice note from Farhan...

Farhan: Oh di! Where are you? We are waiting for u from past 1hour. It is already dinner time and you are not here come soon wherever you are there... we are waiting for you to have dinner together. Come soon.

Detective: Lisa! What is the time? My brother and Hero is calling me for a dinner...

Lisa: Actually it already mid-night the magical world and future world has same time...

Detective: Do one thing give me this diary I will go through it whole night and next morning I will come here and from here we will go the Tommy's home where we will find what we have seen in the pearl... is it ok for you Lisa.

Lisa: Ok! We will meet tomorrow morning...

Detective: Hey! River water can I come out the this place or I have to cross the mountain again...

The river water: Nope! You can come out from here itself...

Detective: Thank you!

Lisa: Meet you tomorrow... byes take care.

Detective: Bye...good night!

I came back to the magical world and I thanked the river water...I was able to listen to some people voice with full alert I turned back it was Hero and Farhan in search of me I think they have my GPS location so they have come here. They came to and started asking so many questions.

Farhan: Di... where was you? We were worried about now tell me where did go?

Hero: Yep! I was also thinking what special work you had that you didn't wanted me to involve...

Detective: Can we go to the palace and speak about all this morning I am really tired. I have no more energy to answer both of your questions...

Farhan: Sure! We will speak about it next morning now let us go...

I can easy change the topic in Farhan's mind but not in Hero's mind he will ask me again and again question me about it until and unless I answer him... we reached the magical palace...I went to the dining area very soon.

Detective: I have eat so much so I can't eat anything.

Hero: Its ok you sit with us until we have dinner...

Farhan: Yep! Di... I will tell you what we enjoyed whole day...

Detective: Sure!

I said myself my god I have to study this diary and revel the secrets of the magical paintbrush and the price less box...these two should never know it. I have to go to the reality I have to solve this by my own...

Hero: Hey! You are somewhere to be lost what are you thinking tell me...

Farhan: Yep! Di... you are not listening to me...

Detective: Actually bhai... I am little bit tired... so let me rest I will listen to you morning... ok! I am going to sleep...good night!

Farhan: Good night!

Hero: Good night!

I moved from the dining hall... hero stopped me from behind.

Hero: Hey! Stop... I just wanted to give you this locket...

Farhan: A locket! Buddy when you purchased it... you didn't say me.

Hero: No I found it near the river where we picked her from ...

I saw the magical pearl was glowing and I want it to be taken from Hero. I was worried then I got some idea of getting of that magical pearl locket.

Detective: Hero... this is the magical pearl locket that revelled all the secrets of the disaster... it was given to me by the river water so I keep it every time with me. See it is glowing give it to me I have to keep it with me or else again disaster may happen...

Farhan: Hey! Buddy give to di... we can't again fight with it.

Hero: Hmm...

Detective: Thank you! And Good night!

I came running and closed my room's door sat on the bed with magnified glass and the locket... I was worried thinking if I would stay there for single more minute and locket would revel all the secret...I heard some noise in my voice translator the conversation held between Farhan and Hero.

Hero: Buddy Farhan! Your di... is trying to hide something from us.

Farhan: I don't think do buddy...

Hero: But I am dam sure she is doing something very secretly I want to find out what is it?

Farhan: Don't worry! She will tell us. Before we verify about it...

Hero: Hmm...

Farhan: Oh! Come on buddy you are thinking so much. Now go to your room rest properly tomorrow morning we will know what is going on...

Hero: Hmm... good night! (Deep thinking voice)

Farhan: Good night! Stop thinking go sleep now...

I remembered that I have keep that voice translator in Hero's bag pack. Hope he have not found it...I came back to work of the magical locket and diary...somebody knocked my door... when I opened the door I found no body out when I turned back hero was sitting on the bed looking at the dairy and the locket...

Detective: What non-sense? What are you doing here at this time? Answer me Hero.

Hero: First answer me. What is matter of this locket...what do you think you can hide this from me... Never!

Detective: You may go now! I have nothing to tell you about this locket.

Hero: Ok! Then tell what this book mean.

Detective: it is just magical story book...

Hero: Oh! Really I really expected the same answer from you... Tell me who is Lisa?

Detective: Who is she? I never heard such name Lisa...

Hero: Yep! I knew that you will give me the same answer. All thanks to my partner who was with you who brought all the information to me.

I was thinking what to say because Hero was speaking about Lisa and I didn't find any more option of sending him back to his room. I got an idea of saying him something so that he believe and go from and stop questioning me about it.

Detective: Cam down there is nothing like that... I have solved the problem behind the magical pearl.

Hero: Oh Really!

Hero removed my watch and showed me some mini voice translator...I was shocking seeing to it. But I knew that Hero don't know more about the magical pearl locket, magical box and magical paint brush...

Detective: It means you listen to me, the river water and Lisa then what else you want to know.

Hero: I just want to what is your next plan... I even know you have to go back to the reality to the Ram charan's home and to know the secrets so tell me when you're going...

Detective: Hero I have not yet decided when to go there? Because I haven't completed this diary and I have promise Lisa...

Hero: you have promise Lisa that next morning you will meet her... tell me where you went...

Detective: Oh! Hero it is very long story.

I said him everything about what happen. How I reached my own paintings... he was listening to me I don't know when slept by listening to me...I used my magical powers and made a blanket to carry Hero to his room... I was back to my work... I was unable to read anytime because I was fully tired when I looked on to the time it was very late but still I tried to keep my eyes open I couldn't so I slept...

Next morning,

Lisa: Wake up! We are already late.

I opened my eyes looked on to the time it was just 2:30 AM... I got up...

Detective: Lisa! It is just 2:30 AM very early. I can't get up (lazy sleepy voice)

Lisa: No! We have to go now itself... or else we may can't go....

Detective: Lisa! What are you saying? Can you tell me properly why can't we go?

Lisa: Actually as we got the warning that the person's life will be in risk after opening the magical pearl locket...

Detective: Yep! So what! We haven't find any risk till now...

Lisa: No don't tell like that. Some monsters attacked on the future world they have even updated some virus in Roberts systems. Really impossible to come out of it... the monster came for me when I didn't surrender to them they tried to destroy the world... I have bring all human beings of future world to magical world so that they will be safe here... now we have to complete the task as soon as possible... or else we can't go...out of this world and reach reality.

Detective: Ok! We will go now itself... or else the monster will follow us to the reality and destroy the reality... you mean to say right!

Lisa: Yep! Let us go...

Detective: Let us go... a prince of the magical world I request you to open the doors to the reality...

We both came to the reality but it was similar to the magical world itself. When I saw all around it was magical world only...my magical powers were not were working... I came back to palace and woke up Hero...

Detective: Hero... Wake up...

Hero: It is only 2:45 why are you waking up so soon. (Lazy sleepy voice)

Lisa: You have to get up or else we will be in problem...

Detective: I think I have lost my magical powers... we have to go the reality and sort out the secrets wake up Hero.

Hero: What! You lost the magical powers...it means as I saw yesterday in the magical temple the paint brush was glowing I thought it is simply glowing it means the magical paint brush gained all the powers again and you lost your powers...

Lisa: We have to go to the reality before all the monsters reach here and any disaster creates here...

Detective: Hero: why can't you try to open the doors of magical to the reality?

Hero: No Madam see even my magic is not working I think I have also lost my powers. Now we have to stop magical paint brush...

Lisa: We can't fight against the magical paint brush. Because it had gain all the magical powers and with powers it can easily bring disaster and defeat us...

Detective: We are not enough to go against to the magical paint brush... so we have to plan something and we have to gather people...

Lisa: But still we can't go against the powers...

Hero: We have no option...other we have plan something very quick... do you anything else.

Detective: We can go the magical river and ask some solution about this problem.

Lisa: Perfect idea! We will go to the river ask some solution.

Hero: Ok! You both go to the river. I will alert people and Farhan to get ready.

We reached the magical river. The river was slowing drying up...

Detective: No! How is possible the river water is slowing drying up.

Lisa: Hey, river water help us out this situation tell us a solution so that we can solve this problem.

The river water: You both have to go to the realty and burn the all paintings done by Ram charan...

Detective: But the doors of the reality are not opening... because I have lost all my magical powers.

Lisa: Is there no other solution to get rid of this problem.

The river water: No! You have no other option...

Detective: Can you say us is there is other way to go back to the reality?

The river water: Yep! I have the other way to the reality... but you should have powers for it.

Detective: I have an idea! The river water is it compulsory that only I should burn all the paintings... I mean to say that can someone else instead of me can do this work of burning the paintings...

Lisa: Oh! Very fab idea... Can we do it?

The river water: I think you can do it...

Detective: Ok! Then I have a person who can help me out of this...

I made a call to the hacker...I felt the only person who can we take out of this situation.

Hacker: Hi... where are you?

Detective: I have no time to explain you all this...but yes! I need your help.

Hacker: Yes! Always ready tell me...

Detective: You have to reach tommy's house and take out the priceless box and burn his entire paintings gallery...

Hacker: But why!

Detective: I have no time to spare for you to explain... just do it.

Hacker: Ok! As you say.

Lisa: What an idea dear? I loved your smartness...

Detective: I think it is not smartness...

The river water: So now you have time to complete your task of diary.

Lisa: My god! We really forgot about it thank you so much to let us remember about it...

Detective: I have even completed the diary task also....

Lisa: when did you complete it?

The river water: you are really fast in doing all this...

I lied to Lisa because I had a doubt is Lisa is with monsters even river water knew it that I am lying...I was looking on to the Lisa was thinking so much...

Detective: What happen? Lisa there is so much of tension on your face...

Lisa: Is it! No.., I am not thinking anything... I think you're worried thinking about the future of this world...

Detective: Oh my god I forgot of about Hero... I have to contact him... or else he will be worried.

I called Hero...

Hero: Hey I was waiting for your call... what is going on... what are you doing? Where are you at present?

Detective: My god! You are questioning me so much wait a minute I will answer your entire questions... have a break give answer to your brain...be clam.

Hero: Ok! Tell me where are you I have to meet you.

Detective: I am reaching magical palace.

Hero: See you there!

When I turned back Lisa was trying to share some signals I guess she is sending signals to monster...Some monsters came to Lisa. I was really shock to see that my doubt was not wrong. I hid behind the tree and recorded all the video... I was able to listen what Lisa is speaking to monsters.

Lisa: Go back! We missed the chance to attack on this world.

Monster: We're so sorry! We could attack but the paintings has been burned.

Lisa: Yep! I know that I think now we have to work on the plan B.

Monster: We will work on it... permit us to go for it...

Lisa: permission granted... go ahead!

Suddenly my phone rings up. Monster were alert coming near to the tree I was praying for the god to help me out. I don't know how I was in the magical palace.

Hero: Hi!

Detective: My god! How did I come here?

Hero: My powers are back.

Detective: Really! My god you saved my life Hero. Thank you so much!

Hero: What happen I mean you were in danger...?

Detective: Yep! Hero as I had a doubt Lisa is with monsters. Because we burned the tommy's painting gallery. So there plan was failed to attack on us. I have this video of Lisa speaking to monster. I don't know who called me at the time when I was trying to know what next plan B is there?

Hero: Sorry! It was me I wanted tell you that you will be in magical palace in few minutes.

Detective: Thank god they didn't see me or else I would be finish... its ok but still I would know there next plan.

Hero: we have to get ready for every side and be alert from all over the world I think your powers are also back...

Detective: Hope so...

Hero: Try once...on this pond I am sure it will work out.

Detective: Hey! Magical pond can you show what Lisa and monsters planning...?

My magic worked out... but the disadvantage is we couldn't able listen what they are speaking actually. I don't what is there next plan.

Detective: We have to be alert and behave normal with Lisa. She should not know that we know she belong to monsters.

Farhan: Lisa is coming! Welcome Lisa.

Lisa: Who are you?

Hero: Oh Lisa! Meet my friend he is Farhan.

Lisa: Hi! I am sorry I have never seen you here so I questioned you in that way.

Farhan: Hey! It's ok. So tell me what your next plan is.

Lisa: Plan! What plan? When did made a plan? Is there any action towards monsters?

Hero: Clam down Lisa. We have not made any plan just waiting for the monsters plan.

Detective: I think the monster have even made plan B because there plan A is failed by me.

Hero: I think we have to be alert because monsters can switch to the human's body I have heard like that from so many people.

Farhan: My god! We have to be so alert. They may be there among us we will not know that itself... We have to prepare for every attack.

Lisa: Yep! We will plan something really twisted so that they will never know what our plan was.

Hero: Sure Lisa! We will plan something that is really difficult to understand.

Detective: Now let us all together have lunch...

Farhan: I am really hungry.

I could see Lisa was tapping on her plate with her fingers... I was dam sure that she trying to share some signals to the monsters...I saw some lady in the kitchen was also doing the same. I observed them I got something special news even that lady was monster who have switch the body and have come here... so that if something happens Lisa will be safe.

Detective: Lisa why are you tapping on the plate. What happen are you alright or you didn't like the food.

Lisa: No I am alright...the food is very delicious...Actually I used to play an music instrument called "piano". I am actually missing it.

Hero: Oh! Is it can you play something me after the lunch.

Lisa: Sure! But where is piano?

Farhan: You don't worry about it. We will get you a piano.

Lisa: Thank you...

We had done with done with our lunch as Lisa wanted to play piano. Hero and Farhan stetted up the piano and etc...I was able to see Lisa was tension. I guess she lied about the playing piano...suddenly she fall down on the floor. I guess she is acting for not planning a piano. We said her to rest.

Detective: Hero there is lady in the kitchen. Who is also with Lisa? You know why Lisa was tapping on the plate?

Hero: Why?

Farhan: It is called tap language she sent some signals to the kitchen lady and lady replied her.

Detective: So Farhan and Hero... we have to make plan now because Lisa is not with us. We have to make 2 different plans. Plan 'A' we have to say

Lisa... and follow the same with her. Plan 'B' This plan is to trap the monsters and fail there plan.

Hero: I have an idea! Listen to me...

Farhan: I think this is may be a plan 'A'. What a fab plan... you are genius Hero.

Detective: Not bad plan! But we have to be care full while working on it...

Hero: Then what about plan 'B'?

Farhan: I have something very interesting plan. Listen to me...

Detective: Superb idea! Now I think we will have success let us do it boys.

Hero: We can do it!

Farhan: Yep! We can do it! Let us go to Lisa and explain our plan.

We all reached Lisa's bed room... she was trying to do something... she was looking to the sky...I kept observing by standing out of the room. I made Hero and Farhan to inside the room.

Hero: Lisa! Listen to me I have made a plan for tomorrow.

Farhan: Yep! We have to go according to the plan.

Hero: so I will explain you what is your role in plan... you and Farhan will be going to the future world and see what is going on... I will be here with Madam getting ready for a war...and we have to even break the magical paint brush so that all this war will not happen in reality...to save reality we have to break magical paint brush... at last your and Farhan's part is to go to magical river get the magical rocks to keep around the magical temple so that if some monster tries to enter the magical temple the magical rocks will guard the temple... this is our plan! What do you say it is enough good to fight against the monster...

Lisa: Oh yes! We will be successful.

I entre the Lisa's room...

Detective: what is going on? You both are here.

Hero: Oh! We discussing about the plan.

Farhan: All set for tomorrow. We are ready...

Lisa: Yep! All set we can do it!

Detective: Now we have to go let Lisa rest for sometimes because she have to go the future world tomorrow.

We came out of the room... I stood there for few minutes Lisa sent signals to the monsters. That's what I wanted to happen? Farhan and Hero reached magical temple as per plan 'B'. Farhan sent me a message of reaching the destination. I reached magical temple. Then as per our plan 'B' we have to make a clone of ourselves. So that after completing the plan A secretly we have to complete the Plan 'B'. We will be in front of Lisa also and our clones will be working on the plan. As we discuss we made our clones... and we were ready to do it...we made our clones to hide in magical temple. Just waiting for next morning...we came back to the palace...

Detective: Hey! Magical ponds will our plan be successful tomorrow isn't it?

When I questioned magical pond...it showed me that our plan will be failed and magical paint brush will take all monsters to the reality and Lisa will take Hero, Farhan and me to show what disaster she will bring...after seeing this I called an urgent meeting.

Hero: What happen? All set right plan is ready we know it will be successful then why this meeting?

Farhan: Yep! Tell us what happen?

Detective: our plan is going to fail I saw it in magical pond. It showed me that our plan is not strong enough against monsters because even paint brush is with them helping out... I think magical paint brush had informed the monsters about our plan...

Hero: What are you saying then we have to think something else now there is no option...

Farhan: My god! Give some idea to my brain.

Everyone sat thinking with me but what to do? We got no idea itself... 3 hours later...

Hero: Hey! Did anybody have any idea?

Detective: Nope!

Farhan: No Hero! My brain is not working to think.

Hero: nobody have any idea about tomorrow. So we have be alert whatever happens tell me...

Detective: Hope we should get some idea till morning.

Farhan: I think we have to ask the river water may it help us.

Hero: Oh what fab idea!

We reached the magical river.

Detective: Hey! River water I need your help...

The river water: Yes! You have come here to make a plan against monsters. Am I right!

Hero: If you know everything why don't you help us out of this instead of wasting the time?

Farhan: Hero polite please you can't speak to the river water like this...

The river water: It is ok he stressed himself by thinking so much about the plan. Don't worry I have a supper plan.

Detective: Tell us the plan please.

Farhan: Hope it will work out.

The magical pearl locket was glowing continuously. I felt there is some monster surrounding us.

Detective: Stop! River water we no need your help...

Farhan: But why? We have no option expect listening to the magical river water.

I started walking all over the river bank walked near the tress that was there near river bank the locket was stopped glowing. When I stepped near the river water the locket was glowing... then I got to know that the river water has turned evil...Hero was standing next to me I whispered in his ears.

Detective: Hey! Hero this river has turned evil if we stay here for more time we will also be turned evil (Whispering voice)

Hero: What! Are you serious? So we have to go from here now.

Detective: Yep!

Hero: Farhan... Farhan! Come here I have some work with you.

Farhan: Yes! I am coming...

We pulled farhan out the river bank and brought him back to the palace. He was questioning a lot but we didn't answer him...

Farhan: Can you both tell me what is going on here? Nobody is answering me what is happening you both are so quite?

Hero: Farhan calm down. I will answer your questions.

We were going inside the magical palace... the pearl locket was glowing so bright that we can't even open our eyes...I got know that monsters have already working on their plan by occupying the magical palace.

Detective: I think we should not go inside the palace.

Farhan: But why?

Hero: No... now don't say even magical palace is occupied by monsters...

Detective: Yep! You are right this magical palace is occupied by monsters.

Farhan: Can one of you tell even me what is going on?

We all reached the magical temple...there the pearl locket didn't glow... Hero used his magical powers and made some invisible trap so that if somebody tries to enter the temple we will be alert by the alerting alarms. We stepped inside temple and cleared all Farhan's doubts...he was really shock to know the truth...

Hero: Hey! What about that diary like book did you completely read it...

Detective: Nope! My god! I have really forgotten about the diary...

I took the diary from my bag pack... started reading it...

Detective: Dear Diary... Today is 10thApril some girl's life I saved today she became my assistant artist...I am really happy to have Lisa as my assistant artist. Oh I didn't write what is the girl's name her is Lisa. She has a good sense of humour...She very pretty to...she really looks like a doll. Oh see have come here I will complete the diary work later.

Hero: Lisa is in this diary also... This is really interesting.

Detective: If Lisa knows Tommy then why did she say me she doesn't know about this artist?

Hero: Can I read the next page?

Detective: Sure! Why not?

Hero: Dear Diary...Today is 12thApril and I lost Lisa in the fair when I tried to track her GPS location. I found her Phone near the old mountain caves where usually people never go... the same way I too returned back from there. But I wanted to save Lisa so I stepped inside I saw there was nothing scary as the people used to say I brought her back but she is not speaking anything as per I know I think she is shock by seeing something really dangerous...

Detective: Really!

Hero: This girl is even acting there... wow!

Detective: Dear Diary...Today is 14thApril and today Lisa spoke to me by say that she have seen some monsters in the cave...but when I asked her how did you reach there she said she saw a lady who really looks like her mom so she followed her and reached the cave... she said me that the lady was trapped by monsters and made her also a monster.

Hero: It means Lisa doesn't belong to monsters. She is just working for monsters to save her mom's life...

Detective: Might be...

Hero: Dear Diary today 16thApril. I conformed that is the lady is missing from the area and even conformed is that lady is Lisa's mother...some monsters came today and took Lisa and attacked on me...but because of the pearl locket I didn't get any injury but the monsters took away Lisa with them. I tried to follow them but failed in it... but I got the magical paint brush again... I am really tied to get rid of this box but I could not...

Detective: My god! The box again came to him...

Hero: A box! Is he speaking about the puzzle box?

Detective: Yep!

I explained Hero all pervious diary notes...he understood everything. Then we moved to the next page there was nothing written over there...the pages were empty nothing was there...

Hero: Hey! What is this? There is nothing else after this page...

Detective: But how is it possible? He must have written something.

Hero: After the page 14thApril there is nothing else.

Detective: My god! How can I forget about it Tommy had a flight to Italy on 16thApril... the same day he was killed.

Hero: Oh Yes! This case is going to close at last and it is time to know who killed Tommy and the case will be solved.

Detective: Yep! Finally we get out this case and close it.

Hero: Wait! Where is Farhan? I have not seen him from past an hour...

Farhan: Hey! Guys actually I was feeling hungry so I brought some fruits for our dinner.

Detective: Oh wow! Smart boy...

Hero: I am really hungry let us eat what you are waiting for...

The locket was glowing when I touched the fruit. It was a wild fruit very dangerous to eat...and Farhan bought it for us... my doubt cleared out Farhan also turned evil.

Detective: Don't eat these fruits Hero. These are wild fruits very dangerous... we can't them. (Whispering voice)

Hero: Oh I was so hungry! But I will change this fruit into to some other tasty food with the help of magic...But why did Farhan bring these fruits for us...

Detective: Coz he has also turned evil... so we have to be careful or send Farhan far from us...

Hero: True! Wait a minute I will send him far from us.

Detective: Do something quick!

Hero: Hey Farhan! Can you stay near the magical palace and get the information about what is going on there. Coz they may get doubt because we didn't go to the magical palace for dinner also... so you go there say the some valuable and cover it up... did you understand what I mean to say you.

Farhan: Yes! I am going you both take care of yourself.

Hero: Bye!

Detective: Not bad Hero! You sent Farhan to the palace. Nice!

Hero: Now tell me what to do next because if we sit here like this tomorrow the war will not stop... so do you have some idea!

Detective: The war will not happen tomorrow.

Hero: How can you say?

Detective: See there is something glowing on the page when I opened it I got the door of reality... we will go to the reality and sort out all secrets and problem will be solved.

Hero: My god! This is a jackpot finally we got the door of reality. But how can we solve the imaginary world's problem in reality...

Detective: As I said you that we have burn Tommy's painting gallery same way we have to burn even my sketches an paintings and the problem will be solved we have to even destroy this magical paintbrush... so problem solves...

Hero: But what about the people who stay here? They will be also the part of destroying the world.

Detective: No people will lose life. Coz we will bring everyone to the reality and kill all evil people and burn all the paintings...

Hero: Will the people will adjust their life in reality.

Detective: I am sure they will because this world will be destroyed then they will have no option.

Hero: Ok fine! Form where shall we start now?

Detective: The people of the future world are here we will start from them.

Hero: But before we shift them there we have to find a place for them.

Detective: Don't worry about it. I made all arrangements with the hacker I found very good place for all these where they can start their new life.

Hero: Oh wow you have done everything! So let us go to the reality and see what the status of it at present. Coz we have not been to home from past 6 days.

Detective: Not 6 days only 6 hours u forgot about the time. The time is not same in reality and imaginary world.

Hero: Oh! Yes I really forgot about it...let us go to the reality and revel all secrets and close this case and save everyone's life.

Detective: Cool! Let us go...

We reached the reality after 6hours as per reality but as per imaginary world it was 6 days. I really missed all my things...we came out of the imaginary magical world and reached the reality. But we came out in someone's room when I looked around it was full of gadgets and computers.

Hero: Whose room is this? The person has all latest model gadgets.

Detective: I guess we are in hacker's room.

Hacker: Hey! Welcome back!

Detective: Hi...Is everything set?

Hero: Hi!

Hacker: Yep! Everything is set...

Detective: So we can start shifting people from there to here.

Hacker: Yep! I have got something very interesting think for you both.

Detective: About what?

Hacker: Mira the scientist the team member of detectives have create some radiation gun that can make a negative thinker person thinking positive so it will help us to kill evil people and make them good and bring them here.

Hero: Wow! What a fab creation?

Detective: Really this is really good.

Hacker: Let us go for a mission kill evils...

Hero: Oh! I am very excited...

Detective: Me too...

We have to go back to the imaginary magical world again...After 30 minutes as per reality we reached the imaginary magical world I tried the radiation gun on Farhan. He became normal same way Hacker and Hero made everyone normal.

Detective: Hey! Everyone this is your creator speaking now the problem of monster has been sort out so you people have to move from here this world is going to destroy so start packing your bags we will have to move from here...

I got everybody's quick response we took everybody to the reality...but I didn't find Lisa. Hacker, Hero and Farhan took everyone to the reality... But I stayed in imaginary world and started searching Lisa.

Detective: Lisa....Lisa! Where are you? This world is going to destroy and you are still here come on... come out wherever you are hiding.

Lisa: I don't want to come to the reality! I know you know I belong to the monsters but still you have come for me...

Detective: Lisa...We have to get out of it...let us go.

Lisa: Nope! I will not come. I wanted to tell you that I got orders from monsters king to kill the great artist Ram charan for his magical paint brush...But unfortunately I didn't get it...I took his diary but I couldn't get what he has written over there coz the locket was with you...

Detective: Lisa... we can even discuss this later now our life is in danger lets go from here.

Lisa: You go... I can't come there coz I am still a monster if the monsters king track me the reality will be in trouble...

Someone pulled me to the doors of the reality...but I wanted Lisa to come with me...

Detective: Lisa you have to come with me. Lisa... come on run hold my hand we will go to the reality...

I reached reality Lisa didn't come with me Hero pulled me out of the imaginary magical world...Farhan and Hacker burnt all the paintings. The imaginary magical world is no more...Everybody was safe but only Lisa...Only her I couldn't take her out of that world.

Hero: The magical paint brush and the priceless box have destroyed itself...I found all the secrets. This is case is going end now.

Detective: Case solved! Lisa was the person who killed Tommy for his magical paint brush.

Hacker: Wow! Case is solved finally...

Farhan: Congratulations team detectives of supernatural you have solve this case in 4 days you had a given 8 days' time...

Hero: Let us have a party celebration.

Hacker: Yep! We have to celebrate this movement...let's enjoy.

Farhan: Yes! It is party time...

Hero: Hey madam! Now what are you thinking the case is solved. It is a party mood let us have fun.

Detective: Ok! Let us celebrate it...

I felt bad for Lisa but I was happy that finally I will know who is Hero? After 2 hours...the celebration was done and we returned home...

Hero: Hey! What are you thinking?

Detective: So finally the case is solved. So what you did you remember your words you said me.

Hero: Off course I remember them...

Detective: Then tell me who are you?

Hero: Not now! Today evening...

Detective: But why today evening? I knew that you are one of my classmates but I am unable to recognize you. I don't know why?

Hero: Oh! I am not your classmates.

Detective: Then what was that conversation held between you and Farhan that day.

Hero: I saw you keeping a voice transmitter in my bag pack so I and Farhan planned to make you fool.

Detective: My god! What a plan?

Hero: Thank you! Today is Hacker's birthday.

Detective: Really! I didn't know about it...

Hero: So evening we will keep a surprise party for his birthday...and a surprise for you too I will tell you who am I? By showing you my secret face behind the mask.

Detective: Are you sure?

Hero: Yep! I am... here is your home arrive.

Detective: Oh!

Farhan: Thank you so much you dropped us to our home.

Detective: Thank you!

Hero: you are most welcome. So today evening at 7:30 PM. Hacker's surprise birthday party.

Detective: You be on time Mr punctual.

Hero: Sure! Bye... Have a good day...

Detective: Wish you the same... Bye...

So finally I will know who is behind the mask...so now I have to decorate the surprise birthday party.

...2hours later...

Entire decoration of the surprise birthday party was done...it was already 6:50PM only 10 minutes more...for 7 'o'clock everything was set Farhan was attending guests and Hero and Hacker arrived. After cake cutting ceremony...

There was funny games everybody were enjoying. I saw Hero secretly going out of the party.

Detective: Hey! Stop Hero...

He didn't even turn back and looked at me... some of the girls pulled me and took me to the party...Hacker was happy coz of all arrangements.

Hacker: Thank you so much! This was one of my best birthdays... I will always remember it...

Detective: It is my pleasure to see you happy.

Farhan: By the way where is Hero? I didn't find him.

Hacker: Yep! Even I have not found him.

Detective: An hour ago he went away without informing any of us...

Hacker: No way it is not possible. How can he go like this?

Farhan: But di... how did you he went away.

Detective: I saw him going out when I stopped him he didn't turn towards me...Just went away.

Hacker: Now what will you do to find him... You don't even know how he looks like?

Detective: You are there know. You know him right!

Hacker: Yes! But ...

Detective: No but nothing! Now my next mission is to find the hero....Mission Finding Hero...

The party was done everyone returned their own home. I too returned my home sat near the window looking at the sky...

3 days later...

Every night I used to sit near window look up to sky but today suddenly someone jumped inside my room through window...I stood with full alert and then I found it was Hero.

Detective: What the hell? You suddenly jumped inside my window...have some manners Hero...there is door to my home you can from there.

Hero: Wow! I really missed your every sentence you speak.

Detective: You broke your promise and where the hell were you these 3days.

Hero: Today I will show this secret face that is behind the mask...

Finally I knew today who is Hero... Finally he will show his identity to me...Hero was trying to remove his mask...

To be continued........

www.ingramcontent.com/pod-product-compliance
Lightning Source LLC
Chambersburg PA
CBHW030625060526
44539CB00042B/754